Little Ben's Life

BERNARD BENTLEY

ILLUSTRATED BY JULIA ANDRZEJEWSKA

outskirts
press

Outskirts Press, Inc.
http://www.outskirtspress.com

Paperback ISBN: 978-1-9772-4768-1
Hardback ISBN: 978-1-9772-4876-3

Illustrated by Julia Andrzejewska © 2022 Outskirtspress. All rights reserved - used with permission.

Outskirts Press and the "OP" logo are trademarks belonging to Outskirts Press, Inc.

PRINTED IN THE UNITED STATES OF AMERICA

This book is dedicated to:

Brian C. Bentley for continually speaking the words of life to me.

A SPECIAL THANKS TO

Letha Wheaton Peoples for your unfailing belief in the success of the Little Ben's series.

And to

Shantay Merry and Chrisanne Sapp for encouraging me to do more than what I had initially intended to do.

ACKNOWLEDGEMENT

Thanks to my lovely wife Natacha Bentley for coming up with the front book cover ideals for Little Ben's Life as well as the front book cover concepts for Little Ben's Pledge and Little Ben's Pledge 2. God has given you a great gift.

CONTENTS

The Early Years

1

NITE NITE TIME

Tucked in by his mother, who was sweet and so dear, Ben did not want to go to bed, and this was quite clear.

Ben did not want to go to bed, so he went to the moon. He brought along rice, his bowl, and his spoon. He had a good meal as he enjoyed the sights: this was much better than going nite nite.

Ben did not want to go to bed, so he went to the sun. He took along hot dogs and fresh hot dog buns. The hot dogs were roasted, the mustard did ooze; this was much better than taking a snooze.

Ben did not want to go to bed, so he went out to sea. He relaxed on the water, and felt the cool breeze. The fish were swimming, his anchor did sink; this was much better than forty good winks.

Ben did not want to go to bed, so he went to a meadow. Behind a pot of gold stood a little green fellow. Placed in Ben's hand was a coin that was yellow. This felt much better than his soft silky pillow.

Ben did not want to go to bed, so he went to the zoo. He thought he would visit an animal or two. He saw monkeys and lions, he saw horses, and sheep, but the best thing of all is that Ben did not sleep.

Ben did not want to go to bed, so he went to the fair. He ate cotton candy and chocolate chip bears. He won lots of prizes, a ship, and a map. This was much better than taking a nap.

Ben opened his eyes and to his surprise, there stood his mother right by his side. "Wake up, little Ben, get yourself clean." Ben said out loud, "What a great dream."

2

WHEN I GROW UP

The teacher stood up and spoke to the group. "Listen close, children, here is the scoop. Class has now started; it is the first day of school. When you grow up, what will you do?"

Ben said, "When I grow up, I will be the police. I'll eat lots of doughnuts and catch all the thieves. I will walk on the beat as the bad guy's retreat. To protect and to serve, to me that sounds sweet."

"When I grow up, I'll work in a shop. I'll make buttons and buckles and nice cashmere tops. I'll sew with a machine; I'll punch with the press. My store will be called "Your Favorite Dress."

"When I grow up, I will go out to sea. I will relax on the water and feel the cool breeze. I'll drink lemonade; I'll spy pirate ships. I will charter a boat and give away trips.

"When I grow up, I'll be a deep-sea diver, a butcher, a baker or maybe a bus driver. I'll drive around town; I'll stop at every bus stop. When people get on, I will point at the fare box. When people are naughty and refuse to pay, when they get off, I will still say, have a nice day.

"When I grow up, I will be a preacher, a prophet, a pastor, or maybe a teacher. I will minister here, and I'll minister there, I will cry out loud and I will not spare. I will tell many people that new life can begin, by confessing Jesus Christ you can live free from sin."

"When I grow up, I will hike in the mountains, I will eat wild berries and drink from cool fountains. I will sleep by the fire and catch fish every day. For me there will be no work and all play."

"When I grow up, I will be a chef; I'll cook almond chicken and roast turkey breast. The mushrooms sauteed, the beef will be stewed, just a taste of delight from the hungry house crew. Free refills on french fries, drink pop until you drop; you will enter and leave still smacking your chops.

"All of these things I would happily be, however, for now, it's just good to be me."

3

NOTHING TO DO

The sun was shining when Ben arrived home from school. Little Ben was bored, he had nothing to do.

Ben was bored so he went to Spain. He walked through the town and ate grapes on the plain. He ate spicy chicken with a side of white rice. Ben found that Spain was a place of delight.

Ben was bored so he went to Seattle. To prepare for the rain, he brought a boat and a paddle. The rain did not stop for goodness sake; some of the puddles in town were the size of a lake. The scenery was beautiful; the trees were so green. The rain was refreshing and kept little Ben clean.

Ben was bored, so he went to Washington, D.C. to see the state's capital and the sweet 'tis of thee. He sat down with the president in a tall leather-backed chair, for an upcoming speech, Ben helped him prepare. Then Ben was excited and went home for the night; he relaxed under the moon until the dawn's early light.

Ben was bored, so he went to Tacoma. He toured the big factories and smelled the aroma. He caught shrimp off the pier; he fished from the shore. Tacoma was a place that Ben just adored.

Ben was bored, so he planted some peas. He watered the flowers and trimmed up the trees. Ben relaxed in the shade of the trees standing tall. He enjoyed the leaves as he watched them fall.

Ben was bored, so he walked in the park. He sat on a beach and he heard the dog's bark. He ate cotton candy and hot apple pie. Ben fed the pigeons as they slowly walked by.

Ben was bored, so he went out to play. He ran through the roses and rolled in the hay. Ben walked by the lake as he took in the sights. He lay in the grass with the sun shining bright.

Ben sat down to rest from an adventurous day. He was plumb tuckered out; he was too tired to play. From Seattle to Tacoma to faraway Spain. From chicken and rice to the cool gentle rain. One thing was good that Ben could not ignore: with an imagination he would never be bored.

4

HOLIDAY

New Year's Day is the start of the year. With cold creamy eggnog and warm family cheer. No problems, no cares, we are full of solutions. On New Year's Day there are fresh resolutions. Say good-bye to the old year, welcome in the new. You have a clean start, now what will you do?

Valentine's Day is a day that is neat. We give cards to our classmates and eat lots of treats. Dad brings Mommy candy with a bunch of red flowers. They go out to eat and don't come back for hours. The babysitter puts us to bed as we slowly count sheep. When Mom and Dad return, we are found fast asleep.

A rainbow, a clover, a shamrock that's cold, a little green man with a pot full of gold. It's St. Patrick's Day with the fresh Irish Spring. You might get pinched if you are not wearing green.

It's Easter, it's sunny with fresh springtime air. Chocolate-filled eggs and marshmallow bears. Bunnies and baskets, the Easter-egg hunt. The green grass in April, what a wonderful month.

On the Fourth of July, what a wonderful sight: to see the fireworks as they light up the night. The sparklers are colorful, the firecrackers are loud. The beautiful show excites the whole crowd.

On October 31st, no ghost and no ghouls. No disfigured costumes that break all the rules. Dress like brave firemen, or angels or clowns. Only those who do good things for people in town.

When you go out at night for no tricks and good treats, remember to ask for something real sweet. When you walk down the street going to and fro, only knock on the doors of the people you know.

The pilgrims crossed over the sea, to arrive on dry land. To help set up the nation as it now stands. The Native Americans were nice and helped them plant corn. The Pilgrims were happy and Thanksgiving was born.

There is turkey, green beans, pie and the dressing, but before you dig in, don't forget to say your blessings. A day to be thankful for family and food, for life, health, and strength and a very good mood.

It's Christmas, it's Christmas, the best time of the year. When people are feeling the holiday cheer. At Christmas we celebrate the birth of our Lord, the sweet gentle Savior whom the world should adore.

There are presents and stockings and a nice Christmas tree, wrapped with bright blinking lights for the neighbors to see. Christmas is a time that the world holds so dear, so have a Merry Christmas and a Happy New Year.

5

SEASONS

Springtime, springtime, the flowers a-bloom, the smell of fresh air, and a breeze through your room. Springtime is nice, it's so sunny and fair; at nighttime Ben sleeps with his soft teddy bear. It is only in springtime that the birds sweetly sing, a melody so nice, what a joy it does bring.

Little Ben likes the summer and the bright blue sky, the smell of the roses and his mom's apple pie. He likes to play catch and tag with his friends. Ben enjoys his new kite as it sways in the wind.

Ben likes the summer because there is no school. No classrooms, no bells, and no tardy rules. He likes the summer with all the good sports, but the only sad part is that summer is too short.

In autumn, Ben relaxes under the trees standing tall. He watches the leaves as they gently fall. Summer is over, soon school will begin, and it's back to the classroom for dear little Ben.

The warm sun is gone, the cold wind is here; soon Ben will find that winter is near. He will put up his tennis shoes and put on his boots, Ben will trade in his play pants for a warm winter suit.

It's winter and little Ben knows the frost is so cold that it bites his toes. It is time to build snowmen and make angel prints, to drink hot chocolate and eat peppermint. Ben slides down the hills on his favorite sled. He enjoys nighttime stories as his mother tucks him in bed.

The Later Years

6

TIME TO EAT

Rise and shine open the blinds fall on your knees and give God some time. From the shadows of night to the light of the sun, nighttime is over, and the day has begun.

The smell of hot bacon floats through the air, as I jump out of the bed and I run to my chair. The table is set, it is in full array it's time to eat breakfast, the best meal of the day. There are grits and eggs sausage and hash browns with creamy hot chocolate to wash it all down. There are biscuits with butter and sweet berry jam with spicy spam patties sautéed in the pan. A good meal in the morning what a great way to start with cold Cap'n Crunch and strawberry Pop tarts. Potato pancakes, crepes and donuts, a blanket of whip cream that is sprinkled with nuts. I like the meats and all the good eats from the cold fresh fruit to the hot cream of wheat. Salads are nice such a healthy delight, but I will take the malt o meal with cinnamon and spice.

Please give me some tea some milk or some juice or maybe some tang for an orbiting boost. Serve me a Pepsi or a cold glass of sprite, I'll even take water with a tart lemon slice. I sit back in my chair and my stomach is full it's time to get dressed and head out to school. I grab a few snacks to put in my pack I am ready for the World and the upcoming tasks. A bright sunny day with the flowers a bloom, a luscious green meadow that has caught by my zoom. Bumblebee's hover over the prestigious green plants overlooking the rows of the elite army ants.

A picnic table a blanket that is spread, a brown woven basket that is full of baked bread. It is time to eat lunch the highlight of the day to fill up my tummy and continue my way. Barbecue chicken is cooked on the grill with smooth zesty sauce it is such a good meal. Hamburgers with onions and hot melted cheese the hunger is now leaving, and my mind is at ease. Soup and salad, rice and red beans, turnip, mustard and sweet collard greens. From the smoky kielbasa with the fresh bean sprouts to the Coney Island hotdogs with the rich sauerkraut. I love the outdoors such a great getaway I can eat in the mountains or dine by the bay. Chili with cheese and fried chicken wings, fire cook prawns and crisp onion rings. Shrimp is my favorite I love it deep fried with pasta and white rice gently place on the side.

Cooking and eating it all equals chores so you do the dishes and I'll eat the s'mores. Crispy graham crackers with melted chocolate, fluffy marshmallows with sweet coconut. Cooked to perfection on a big open flame my hunger is gone, and my stomach is tame.   The stars shine So bright on this wonderful night such a welcome addition to the bright city lights. From the moonlit town to the ocean edge, a comfortable chair overlooking the ledge. Nighttime has come and the fun has begun, the day has now ended because the work is all done.

A fine dining restaurant with a tall leatherback chair, a picturesque view with candles a glare. Pearl white tablecloths with shiny gold plates, tuxedos, gowns and a gorgeous landscape. Long velvet drapes envelope the place with the sleek baby grand and a Tiffany vase. It's dinner it's dinner it is time to eat, from the sweet tasty treats to the savory meats. Grill tenderloins steamed clams and crab cakes, Fried grilled prawns and tender beef steak. Rock salted prime rib with filet mignon the sweet spicy flavor of the chicken Dijon. The atmosphere is nice, and the timing is right, to enjoy a good meal and to welcome the night. The porterhouse steak is a meal made for two, with hot cheesy bread and vegetable stew. Good tender veal with roasted lamb chops a tall glass of lemonade, good to the last drop. Spinach cream corn and the fresh leafy greens, steamed asparagus with the smoky baked beans. The smoked chicken penne and the smooth lobster bisque, the delicious flavor of the fire grill fish.

Such incredible food what I can say from the rise of the sun to the end of the day. Now back to my bed, toasty warm and tucked in. At the Dawn of the day, it starts all over again.

Thankful to God my love from above who is tough like an ox but sweet like a dove. Please watch over me during the darkness of night and I promise to trust you when the sun is shining bright.

7

SEATTLE

Seattle Seattle the Emerald City with deep green valleys and tall Douglas trees. A city so vast yet close to the shore, with sun sent from heaven by the one who adores. There are snow covered mountains, such a beautiful site, with the lavender fields that glow during the night. From the green ponder fields to the deep Puget Sound, where the cockles and mussels are strewed on the ground.

From the great Lake Washington with the I-90 floating bridge to the Fremont troll that sits under the ridge. This city is amazing unique from the rest being put to the test you arise as the best. Take the I-90 freeway or the 405 way, while the Washington state ferry helps you escape for the day. To Whidbey or Vashon for a good Island view, or retreat to Bremerton for some hot seafood stew. Bremerton naval base is a graveyard of ships, deactivated and recycled at the pier they just sit. No nuclear warheads with the radiation waves, no active drills with the D day parade. Just retired vessels tied off at the hip, it's true what they say loose lips do you sink ships.

I am hungry I'm hungry I need to eat, a salad sounds nice

but I want some meat. A hot Dick's burger with greasy french fries or maybe Ezell's with the buffalo sized thighs. Ivar's on the pier is such a delight while Salty's on Alki always cooks it just right. From the spicy chicken wings of my dear chick'n fix, to Beths cafe' with the 12 omelet dish. There is the oyster bar where you eat in your car and at night you can see the bright shooting stars. There's Ruth Chris, John Howie and Stanley Seafort's. They have incredible meals that you eat with a fork. Filet mignon with lamb liver stew so tender and tasty, that you don't have to chew. Garlic mashed potatoes with stout asparagus spears, good from the start until the end of the year.

I am thirsty I am parched I need to wash it all down. Some cold Welch's grape juice, now how does that sound? Give me some water as clear as can be or maybe a cup full of English style tea. Cranberry juice gives me such a good boost. I loosen my belt and take off my shoes. I am winding down it has been a long day, off to the house to pray and to stay. First, I need cookies, cake or ice cream perhaps a piping hot donut from the sweet Krispy Kreme. Ice cream is what I select. There are so many choices, but which is the best? With Cold Stone Creamery you can't go wrong. Put a tip in the jar and they will sing you a song. Salt and Straw is very unique. With so many special treats it is hard to beat. Sub Zero ice cream, it is 30 below. It chills your tongue as well as your fro. A nitrogen system that is state of the art. It freezes your brain but warms up your heart.

The hydroplane races, the torchlight parade, and a walk around Green Lake on a hot summer day. The Seattle marathon with the 26.2 the hot chocolate race is nice, but this one will do. Over 26 miles on the sleek Seattle streets. Gatorade is your companion and gu is your treat. At 18 miles you are more than halfway there, no issues or cares but watch out for the bear.

So many people have made this their home. From the split-level house to the concrete kingdom. There is Bruce Lee, Jimi Hendrix and the rockstar Kurt Cobain but the sax of Kenny G helped seal it's great fame. There is Terry Metcalf who is simply the best with the leather football he would outrun the rest.

The Seahawks the Sounder's the kraken will do, but the Seattle storm will rise like the dew. A group of young women who have soared to great heights WNBA champions they won it all thrice. No fortune or fame tell me who knows their names? They are unknown young ladies with the media to blame. Give them some credit and pay them they're worth, they work just as hard as any other sport. Being a woman is not a set back. They should be treated with respect they don't live in the past. I almost forgot we have a baseball team, but winning a game is more like a dream. A four-leaf clover an oasis Mirage, sticks prop up a house, what a clever façade. We get good players that we don't plan to keep. We pay them big money then we trade them real cheap. We build up our rivals from our farming league. While winning a pennant is more than a tease. To the ball game we go with the tailgating show. To our seats in the middle of the very last row. Hotdogs, candy, pop, and some chew. Do you have peanuts? OK I'll take two. No worries no pressure as a matter of fact, it's easy to be calm when your team is dead last.

From the Pike's Place Market with the fast-flying fish, to the tall Space Needle with the sharp shiny tip. Seattle is wonderful! There is so much to do. From the African Museum to the Woodland Park Zoo. Kerry Park has such a great view overlooking the ferris wheel with the seat built for two.

Take me to Leavenworth that old Germantown or to the Ballard Locks that drinks from the Sound. From the Snoqualmie Falls with the cool gentle mist to the waterfront stores with my favorite dish. The landscape in Seattle is such a gift from above. Sitting under the clouds that are shaped like white doves. Bright blue skies as far as you can see, I will look in the vast and mysterious sea.

The Amtrak train goes straight through the town. It is as quick as the wind without making a sound. Over the river and through the woods, past the log cabin of dear Mrs. Hood. Uber, Lyft and the yellow taxi, electric skateboards and the bike made for three. Transportation is available all over town with the Orca card it can get you around.

You have traveled to Seattle the best place I have found where the sound of heavy rain is heard year-round. Where family is important, it takes center stage like the star-studded cast at the end of a play. The landscape, the events, the great things to do. Like greeting your friends with a sweet toodaloo.

So long my friends. I'll see you next time with a series of rhymes that are cast just in time. Stand up, and give Christ the praise from the set of the sun to every new day.

8

TIME TO TRAVEL

From the small shallow stream that runs past my house, to the powerful river with the big open mouth. From the industrial bay with the massive tugboat, to the prestigious castle with a deep dirty moat. I love the water the big open seas, the screech of the seagulls as they glide through the breeze.

The Arctic ocean is as cool as can be, north of the pole it is the smallest of the seas. The water is slushy with big bergy bits a clever disguise for the sharp iceberg tips. Where the well dress penguins inhabit the land with the white polar bears that are huge when they stand. From the whales and sea lions to the gentle walrus that gigantic creature with the ivory tusk. Weighing 2000 pounds with thick blubber skin long wire whiskers and triangular fins. Feeding on mollusk, crustaceans and fish, where ice-cold worms are their favorite dish.

A sweet fishing hole, a getaway spot, a land that's unknown that time has forgot. I can go to the ocean and fish from the shore or drop in a crab pot to the ocean floor. The lake by my house is famous for trout. It has bass with the big wide mouth. The perch, the bluegill, and sardines a few. Cooked on the fire or boiled in a stew. Mussels and clams a big gooey duck straight from the sand with no feathers to pluck. That crab that crab was made for my mouth, with Cajun style sauce from the deep dirty south. From the cold king crab which is the catch of the day to the colorful blue crab in the warm sunny bay. Crab is my favorite and it is still number one; barbecue boiled or seasoned and spun. The calm green sea and the stiff eastern breeze the horn from a boat and the smell of seaweed. The sea is incredible! A whole different place vast in it's nature like the deep outer space. Exciting and mysterious but virtually unknown yet shelter to many who call it their home.

A dense green forest with a rocky terrain, an ice covered stream with a snowy white plain. The big outdoors is such a great getaway. A break from the stress of the routine workday. From the moss on the ground to the high treetops from the dew on the earth with the gentle raindrops.   The forest is beautiful a place I adore from the cave in the hills to the log cabin doors. So peaceful, quiet, calm and tranquil. No deadlines to meet and no managing bills. No board room meetings with high-leather backed chairs or angry officials with executive stairs. No days, months or years, time seems to stop. No watches and cell phones or loud alarm clocks. Where the crow of the rooster welcomes the day and the howl of the wolf will tuck you away. Where the army ants are the talk of the town, they are the leaders of insects that crawl on the ground.

A reptile, a lizard, a mongoose, a snake, a waterproof tent with the big wooden stakes. Life in the forest is unique from the rest. It stretches your limits and puts you to the test. A day full of work without comfort and ease. No shiny remotes with flatscreen TVs. No La-Z-Boy chairs or deep soaking tubs. No three happy friends with the rub a dub dub. No way to escape from the hot humid day. No insect repellent that really keeps them away. The bright campfire is the greatest highlight, it warms up your tent and pierces the night. From the hotdogs on the flame to the fire grill roast, the smell of this meal seems to sneak up the coast. Graham crackers, marshmallows, chocolate and more; what is this meal? Well, it sounds like a s'more. Cooked at night on a big open flame, my mind has been changed, I will not be the same. Give me the outdoors with the monsoon type rain. The deep green valley in the wide-open plains. You can have the condos, the subways, and the cars. I'll take the mountain with the moon and the stars. You take the rush-hour with the big traffic jams, the capacity crowds where there is no room to stand. I like the hammock with the birds in the trees, the bees on the flowers and the soft little breeze.

A corner office with a cherry wood desk a three-piece suit with a nice velvet vest. A plaque on the wall that says you're the best to you it's a dream to me it's just stress. Oh, give me a home where I'm not all alone, where my best friend is not the TV or the phone. Where all lives matter from the greatest to the least. From the man in the suite to the wild savage beast.

A Fiddler, a cow, a man on the moon. It's just me little Ben with my bowl and my spoon. From a planet called Pluto to the great planet earth to the shock in the galaxy from a star that is birthed. From the brightest star in the deepest of night to my nice little room with the little night light. Millions of stars and planets galore a vast universe for me to explore. Saturn is known for it's three shiny rings the particle flow and the light that it brings. With hydrogen helium and big chunks of ice, this halo shaped mass stands out in the night. Uranus is unique in this northern divide it is tilted at an angle and rotates on its side. Mercury is small yet close to the sun hot like the desert with scorching hot fun. I like Jupiter with its big massive size, it is larger than most planets, but there is no place to hide. It is desolate, and lifeless with a big red spot. Hurricane winds that spins like a top. A cold lonely planet with no sites to see no oceans to sail and no Douglas fir trees. No people or creatures not even a drone, a gigantic planet but nobody's home.

Meteor's, astroids with a cluster of stars, M & M candy and the Milky Way bar. From the orange hot sun that is light years away. Our planet inhabits the vast Milky Way. From the deep outer space where gravity stops to the earth's atmosphere where the meteors pop.

Sit back and relax grab your chair and hold on tight you are about to experience the best show of your life. The moon shines so bright as it reflects the sunlight while the fast-shooting stars disappear in the night. The Aurora Borealis with its colorful scheme, it seems like I am sleeping but this isn't a dream. The deep outer space is for you to enjoy. It is better than games or manufactured toys. Mysterious exciting interesting, and new. A place known by many but experienced by few.

9

SNOQUALMIE

A city, a town, a good getaway. A nice town to visit and a great place to stay. Snoqualmie, in the pacific northwest such lovely landscape it is simply the best. From the twilight night to the rise of the sun. From the beast in the east to the west that was one. There is luscious green grass and white waterfalls, wild bobcats with thick padded paws. Lions and tigers and bears oh my, chewy beef jerky and huckleberry pie.

Tall Douglas firs and steep mountainsides. White capped mountains with the northern divide. A place of serenity comfort and peace where the sweet sound of silence can calm the wild beast. I love the meadows and the slow gentle streams the kind that you find in a beautiful dream. A vast green valley with snow covered slopes. A bright shooting star that is seen through my scope. A nice soft breeze that can put you at ease with the sway of the trees and the sound of the sea.

Snoqualmie, such a wonderful place the great outdoors with an abundance of space. From the big log cabins which are made from wood. To the modern day homes which are fab but still good. Away from the hustle and bustle of town. With noise all around and trash on the ground. Where peace and quiet is just hard to find, like a rhyme out of time or an empty gold mine. The taxi's the Ubers, the people on bikes. No beautiful sights it just doesn't seem right. There are thick crowded streets with no place to retreat with construction sites on every Main Street.

Where are the mountains, the valleys the trees the vast blue skies and the wide-open seas. The people that share and the families who care the bright red signs that say don't feed the bears.

The rivers the streams and the colorful dreams. Life may look bleak but it's not what it seems. With life comes opportunity and a glimmer of hope. A way of escape from the end of your rope. Just trust in the father, the ancient of days the Alpha and Omega who has open the way.

To the Salish lodge for a wonderful stay, three or four nights is a good getaway. A stone fireplace with marble countertops, an 80-inch screen and a mini laptop. A hard-wood floor with crystal glass stalls, a picturesque window overlooking the falls.

Eat in the restaurant or dine in your room whichever you like it is all up to you. Fresh whipped potatoes with tender lamb chops, to add asparagus puts you over the top. This delightful food can settle your mood but please don't forget the Mulligan stew. Oysters on the half shell to add to the lamb, sure I'll take a slice of the holiday ham. I'm stuffed I am so full it's time to go to sleep but first let me have a sweet nighttime treat. Please give me some blackberry, or huckleberry pie, with a scoop of vanilla ice cream placed on the side. Moist carrot cake with icing on top, I am licking my plate and smacking my chops. Some ice cold water to wash it all down, or maybe some lemonade, now how does that sound. Tarte cran-berry is my favorite juice squeezed straight from the fruit it always gives me a boost.

Cedar and Adam are skiers extraordinaire, from pounding

the moguls to catching big air. They cut through the powder with skis like sharp blades, the snowy white spray with the crowd all amazed. With the top of the trees just under their skis, please don't try to compete, these two can't be beat. From the start of the day until the sun goes down up on the slopes is where they'll be found. A race to the bottom as fast as they can. They cross the finish line and they beat their old man.

The town of Snoqualmie is a place that I adore from the Columbia river to my wood carved door. Such great scenic beauty for family and friends for people who travel and the closest of kin.

If you need some relief from the wild rat race from the eight-hour day with a 30-minute break. From the crowded subways and the cramped little cars to the dark oyster bars with the ceiling of stars. Come to the town that time has forgot, where the children are taught, and love can't be bought. Where nature is treasured from the birds to the bees to the cool gentle breeze and the tall cedar trees. A place of laughter love and good cheer, from the very first month until the end of the year.

10

MY DREAM

I dream of a place where mansions aren't sold, where streets are pure gold and you never grow old. Where everyone, is dressed for the town, with Fluffy white gowns and shiny gold crowns. I dream about peace from the west to the east from the king in the castle to the lad on the street.

No worship of money or goods that are sold. No hot melted gold that is poured in the mold. No fortune or fame that is fit for the flame, but a precious white stone with a holy new name.

I dream of a place where there is no fear, No anger and violence with uncontrollable tears. Where cops don't need Glocks to stop and to drop. Where the doors are wide open with no master locks. I dream of a place where there is perfect peace. Where you rest from your labor and your mind is at ease. No sunshine of day or moonshine of the night because the Lord of all Lords is the only true light.

A majestic home, a rainbow, a throne. A perfect foundation with the chief cornerstone. Wonderful and excellent in all of your ways. You are the Alpha and the Omega, the ancient of days. You descended from heaven, like a sweet gentle dove. You gave us a gift then you ascended above. White woolly hair with eyes like a flame, exalted above all is your heavenly name. Your voice is like water and your feet like fine brass. You can't be compared to the shiny gold calf. A silk golden sash is tied off at your waist. A gentle reminder of your love and your grace. Faithful and true is how you are known from the top of your throne to every true home.

"Little Ben's Life" is a fun and entertaining book suitable for all readers. Written in rollicking rhyme it is sure to capture your attention. In the early years Ben overcomes boredom and life's challenges by using his vivid imagination as a way of escape. While in the later years Ben shares his incredible experience of living in the Great Pacific Northwest.

ABOUT THE AUTHOR

The author is the Pastor and founder of Latter Rain International Church. He received his start as a model for Elan Modeling Troupe. Bernard later went on to act in several films. He is focused on continuing his work as a writer and pursuing his passion of filmmaking. He speaks English, Tagalog, Spanish and Haitian Kreyol. Bernard has over 30 years' experience in martial arts.

CPSIA information can be obtained
at www.ICGtesting.com
Printed in the USA
JSHW012329270222
23271JS00002BA/6